I0520130

OWN YOUR TRUTH SERIES

Book II

Just Us Two-A Novella

Always and Forever

Just Us Two - A Novella
Always and Forever

PUBLISHED & DISTRIBUTED BY
B'ARTFUL, LLC

April 2016

All inquiries should be made to Michelle Morgan Spady.
No part of this book may be reproduced or may, in whole
or in part, by any means, transmitted in any form or by
any electronic or mechanical, including photocopying,
recording, or by any information storage or retrieval
system, without permission in writing from the publisher.

ALL RIGHTS RESERVED.

ISBN 13: 978-0-9914600-6-9
ISBN 10: 0-9914600-6-5

Library of Congress Control Number:
2016906550

Printed in the United States of America

Copyright © 2016 Michelle Morgan Spady
www.michellespady.com

This novella is a work of fiction. Names, characters,
places and incidents are either the product of the author's
imagination or are used fictitiously. Any resemblance to
actual events, locales, organizations, or persons living or
dead is entirely coincidental and beyond the intent of
either the author or the publisher.

Also by Michelle Morgan Spady

Enough was Never Enough
Book One-OWN YOUR TRUTH SERIES

Kiana S.M.A.R.T. for Class President

ShoozyQ and the AB Crew in Bully on the Playground

An Artist and His Obsession (Co-Author)

7 Days 2 Tell

Contributor

The SIDS Survival Guide
Joani Nelson Horchler & Robin Rice

Legendary Locals of McLean (Featured)
Carole L. Herrick

Two Minutes
The Great Falls Writers Group

Just Us Two-A Novella
Always and Forever

MICHELLE MORGAN SPADY

A.O.S. – Always and Forever - B.O.S.

In loving memory

Of

My mother

Flora Futrell Morgan

My inspiration - My rock - My strength

Just Us Two

Chapter 1

Jade and Porter

"Happy New Year, Mr. Grey!" Jade said to Porter. She felt so safe whenever his arms were wrapped around her.

"Happy New Year to you, Mrs. Grey!" He pulled her tighter to him.

Married not quite a month, both of them were still giddy from the newness of it all, or it could've been the Veuve Cliquot champagne their bodies had consumed since early evening. There was no one else in their world right now. Just Mr. and Mrs. Potarius Maxwell Grey. As far as Jade was concerned, it could go on forever like this. She loved the sound of her new name, even though she still hadn't quite decided if she would use it for business purposes. This bothered Porter because he wanted her committed to him fully, and that meant carrying his name. Whenever the topic would come up, Jade changed the subject or used the excuse of legal business reasons to keep using her own name. But none of that was important right now. She finally had her man where she wanted him, right in her arms on New Year's Eve. No Porter's four-year-old, Addie. No crazy sister, Lynn. As Jade always said, "Just us two," taken from the title of the song by her all-time favorite artist, Teena Marie.

"Porter, let's promise to keep our love new and full of life like this for the rest of our lives," she said, laying her head on his broad shoulders and closing her eyes as tightly as she could. Luther Vandross' version of the song Always and Forever played loudly over the speakers as they danced as if they were the only two on the dance floor. That Tom Ford cologne she had given him as one of his Christmas gifts was working its magic on her at this moment. She could feel every muscle in his body as they began to melt into one another.

"Baby, I promise to keep you safe and love you for the rest of my life," He mumbled, as he moved his tongue in and out of her ear. She always melted when he did that.

"Ladies and gentleman, the clock is just about to strike that bewitching hour. Would everyone please lift your glass and hug that special one you came with or find someone near." This remark brought laughter from the audience.

"Ten, nine, eight…" shouted the party host. Jade couldn't believe she and Porter had made it through another year. She looked up at his smiling face; she had never seen him so happy.

"Four, three, two…ONE! Happy New Year!" the party host finished. Black and gold balloons and confetti dropped from the ceiling and filled the room. Jade and Porter clicked their glasses and quickly set them down so that they could freely embrace and kiss as they never had before. This was it. Always and forever.

Porter began squeezing Jade's hand in his. "Mrs. Grey, would you join me upstairs in the suite?"

"My pleasure, Mr. Grey; by all means, lead the way."

They couldn't keep their hands off each other as they made their way to the elevator, a perfect haven to start what was about to happen in the suite. Luckily, there was no one else inside because they would not have been able to withstand the heat that was generated between the two of them.

Porter leaned against Jade gently, but firmly, as he pushed her hair back and began kissing her neck. It ended all too abruptly when the elevator reached their second floor room in what seemed like nanoseconds.

They walked out of the elevator, so close together that they could barely put one foot in front of the other, kissing and hugging all the way down the hall to their suite.

"Excuse me, sir," said another patron of the hotel as he almost bumped into them both.

Porter and Jade laughed heartily as they stopped for a minute to take advantage of one of the walls that was strong enough to hold their weight. He backed her up against the wall as they both embraced and their breaths became quicker and heavier.

"Oh, Porter… please, let's get to the room," Jade whispered in between breaths, her eyes closed. Porter could barely speak as he tried to pull himself back from what he knew would be worth waiting for.

They regrouped and rushed down the hall to Suite 1212, the best suite in the whole hotel. Nothing but the best for both of them. Porter quickly touched the key to the wall to open the door to nothing but grandeur. The hotel guest services had already been by, placed the Swiss chocolates on the bed, and dimmed the lights. Someone must have known that they were in love and would be coming in ready for action because the sounds of Luther Vandross' "For Only One Night" could be heard very softly playing from the iPod on the nightstand.

"Shower?" Porter asked Jade as he quickly closed the door.

"Yes, babe. Let's," Jade purred back at him.

Before they began to undress each other, Jade pushed Porter onto the king size bed which gave them plenty of playground. In between giggles, they touched lips and promised themselves to love each other for life, no matter what.

"Ya think anybody can hear us?" Porter asked in a Barry White bass voice.

"I couldn't care less!" responded Jade as she moved her body up and down his. She began to take off his bowtie as he slowly unzipped her beautiful red gown, the gown which had been hugging her body tightly all night long. The stretchy material shimmered in the dark like stars on a starlit night. The zipper was long, which heated things up when Porter began to pull it down. He had complimented her the entire night on how good she looked.

"You know I've wanted to take this dress off all night, don't you?" He just couldn't help himself and slowly pulled it off of her, carefully tossing it onto the chair in the corner of the room.

He pushed her back on the bed, kissing, touching, biting, and exploring every inch of her body with his mouth, his tongue, and his hands. It had been years since they had made love this way because it seemed that there was always someone in the house.

Jade had never felt freer in her entire life. Immediately she forgot about everything. She was not prepared for this moment. She felt on the verge of an explosion. Their bellies touched and tightened in response to what was taking place. There was a tingling sensation that was going through her neck, arms, and hands as she grasped the covers. Their bodies were writhing and thrashing about, almost to the edge of the bed. Their breaths were rhythmic and in synch.

Porter, being his normal, smooth, cool self, forced her to follow his lead and take it slow. He was denying her and forcing her to yield and enjoy each passionate moment. Every move between them was fervent, urgent, desperate. Again and again, he took her almost to the brink of implosion and then eased her back.

Like an animal who had just captured a primal dinner catch, he devoured her lips and explored her mouth with his tongue.

Within moments, they were fully undressed and in the shower. Porter turned the faucet to hot, but the water was not nearly as hot as the heat that was coming from their bodies. Fully engaged with each other, they hadn't taken the time to hit the fan button on the wall—the light, either, for that matter. Without the fan on, the steam from the shower quickly consumed the bathroom. The only glow in the bathroom was from the fire that they had started with their bodies and the dim light that guest services had left on.

It was almost as if they couldn't decide if they wanted a shower or to be in the tub as they very cautiously eased themselves down into the huge, round jacuzzi that was surrounded by a marble platform and battery-operated scented candles at each corner. The fragrance in the bathroom was like a bouquet of Japanese cherry blossoms, tantalizing to the senses. As Porter held one arm around Jade, he switched the shower off and then touched the button to plug the drain so that the water would start filling up in the tub around them. There was a mirror on the ceiling above the tub, which gave them a full view of their actions. They could still hear the playlist streaming softly through the speakers in the bathroom.

"Wait, babe…please," Jade whispered in Porter's ear as she wrapped her legs around his waist. "I want this to last forever."

He gently pulled each one of her legs from his sides and took a moment just to observe what attracted him to her in the first place, above and beyond her mind, humor, and outwardly physical beauty. After a passionate kiss, he moved away and rested his back against the tub as she sat up and joined him. He pulled her towards him and leaned her against his chest as she wrapped her legs around his body again. The tub was filling fast. They had almost forgotten that Porter had plugged it up. He reached over and shut off the water. It was just enough to cover both their backs and reach their shoulders. Jade placed her head on his shoulder and under his neck as he embraced her, feeling every muscle in his body pressing against hers. She touched the button to turn on the jacuzzi, that was located behind Porter's neck, and the vibrations of the water helped them dissolve with pleasure. They held each other as if there was a possibility of them drifting apart in the tub. Panting, Porter reached down to let the water out of the tub, climbing out first and then turning to help her out. She grabbed a towel and started wiping him off as he returned the gesture, stopping to kiss in between each wipe. Then they eased into the bed where they embraced and peacefully slept until morning.

Chapter 2

Lynn and Casey

"Happy New Year, baby!" Casey whispered in Lynn's ear.

Returning the sentiment, Lynn couldn't be happier. "Happy New Year, Casey!"

Casey pulled Lynn closer, putting his arms around her and laying his head on her shoulder. "I can't think of any other place I'd rather be than lying here next to you. This will be our year."

Lynn cozied under Casey's right arm and pondered those words. *This year will be our year.* She wasn't really clear on what Casey meant, but she had some plans of her own as far as their relationship was concerned. "So, Casey, are you saying that you'd like to take what we have to another level?"

He pushed away from her so that he could see her face as he stared into those beautiful, inquisitive brown eyes of hers. "That's exactly what I'm saying. I've never been this happy in my entire life. I feel so free when I'm around you; besides, I practically live here anyway."

They both laughed.

"You've got that right, mister!" Lynn nudged his side with her elbow. Lynn thought she'd better take advantage of this moment to see what she could do to assure that he remembered his words. She pulled him back to her and pressed her lips against his, tasting the sweetness of his breath as their tongues began to tango.

She believed that she loved Casey, but lately, she had been having so many dreams and thoughts about Gabe, which was totally unexplainable. This was the only topic of conversation that could cause any friction between them. They had had many conversations about this because Lynn never wanted to hide anything from Casey. But for some reason, she just couldn't let Gabe go despite the fact that the airline had confirmed his death years ago. A body was never found, but the official report said that he was burned beyond recognition. There was no way he could've survived that fire. The case was closed.

Jade had suggested that she not go down to the scene because she felt that Lynn would never forget it. Gabe had family in Florida and assured her that they would take care of everything, and when she was ready, they would help her to plan a memorial service for him. Lynn wasn't sure if the dreams were happening because she never really had closure or if it was Gabe coming to her in her dreams asking her to move on with her life or never to remarry.

Her thoughts were interrupted when Casey murmured, "How about we grab a bite to eat?" in her ear.

Maybe he could read her mind and knew that she was thinking about Gabe again. Lynn knew he probably just wanted to distract her from her thoughts. "Sure, I'll beat you downstairs," she said as they both hopped out the bed, grabbed robes, and headed for the bedroom door. Lynn stopped when her phone started to ring. One mind told her just to let it ring; however, she always liked to answer her phone because she never knew if it was an emergency or not, and worst case was if it was her sister, Jade.

"Hello? Hello? Who is this? Why won't you say something?" Lynn quickly clicked off her phone. Another anonymous phone call. This was beginning to annoy her. At first, she thought that it could be Casey playing games with her, but she soon brushed that aside, especially at moments like these when he was right there with her.

"Who was it?" asked Casey as he stopped and turned to look at her.

"Nobody…again," she answered despondently.

They continued downstairs and had their midnight snack of fruit and cheese. Lynn kept her phone close in her pocket.

Chapter 3

Jade and Porter

The Hay Adams hotel was one of the finest five-star hotels in Washington, DC. Porter and Jade almost felt guilty for spending the night and money when they lived only twenty minutes away in Great Falls, Virginia. But it was well worth it to get away from Addie, Lynn, and the rest of the family. Besides everything at work was still slow this time of year, with the holidays and all. In a few hours, they would be packing to head back home, but until then, the night was theirs. They were going to take advantage of every single minute.

"Morning!" Jade whispered to Porter, nibbling on his ear, "Do we have to leave? I'd love to lie here with you all day. Why don't we just extend the stay?

We could get food and come back to bed and finish where we left off. Last night was everything that I had ever dreamed of with you."

Porter gently took her face in his hands and kissed her forehead, cheeks, and then planted a long kiss on her lips. "Morning."

It was only moments before that Jade had crawled back on top of him to receive all that he could give her. In a matter of seconds, the lilac panties she had been wearing were tossed aside. The heat of passion coming from both their bodies was enough to light up all of D.C. Moments seemed like hours as they covered every inch of the king size bed. The moans and groans of ecstasy were at a bare minimum so as not to share their intimacy with any neighboring hotel guests.

"I love you so much!" Jade whispered as her legs tightened around his back to draw him even closer to her.

"I love you, too," he said as he covered her mouth with his, and brushed her hair back with one hand, holding her tight with the other.

Before they knew it, an hour had passed, and the room phone was ringing. They both jumped as Porter grabbed the phone. "Porter Grey."

It was the hotel operator. "Mr. Grey, did you need to extend your stay?" Check out time was 11:00 a.m., and he knew it; however, he looked at his watch and noticed that the time was 12:30. Where had the time gone? That was how it was and had always been with Jade. "Ah, yes, as a matter of fact, if the room is vacant, we will take it for another night," he replied, glancing over at Jade with a sly grin on his face.

Jade radiated with excitement when she heard this revelation. She pulled the beautiful beige satin sheets up around her body and sat up close, holding him around his waist as he handled the situation. That was one thing she loved about Porter; he knew how to take charge and handle a situation. Upon hearing that the room was indeed vacant, he said, "That's fabulous! Thanks, and what's your name? I'll make sure to stop by the desk and show you my gratitude." He finished the conversation with the hotel staff and laid back down, picked up the remote and began flipping through the channels on the television.

This was just what the two of them needed, some down time away from family and friends. They had gone through so much the year before. So many things, like the stunt that Lynn had pulled at the hotel. Though Jade had told Lynn that they were moving past that, it was something she would never forget. She was still digging herself out of that hole with the public, but today was not the day to think about any of that. She was at one of the most luxurious hotels in all of Washington, D.C., lying beside the most handsome man in the world, and she was going to enjoy every last minute of it. Porter grabbed her, pulling her close as she snuggled into his arms and closed her eyes.

Chapter 4

Jade

"Send her in, Brooke," Jade answered into the speaker phone. Two weeks had passed, and she was back at work. Business as usual. It didn't matter because she and Porter had just spent the best holiday ever together. This was a new year, and she was looking forward to new and exciting things as Mrs. Potarius Maxwell Grey, not to mention her new role of stepmother to his little girl Addie.

Brooke was used to that tone since she had been working with Jade for so long. She admired her for all that she had accomplished which helped her to cope with many of Jade's idiosyncrasies.

"By the way, Brooke, did you ever get that appointment for me with Dr. Joe Hamilton?" Jade had promised her sister, Lynn, that she would make an appointment to see the psychiatrist, Dr. Joe Hamilton, after her wedding. It was part of the bonding for them. Not only was it for Jade to get clarity and talk out some of her issues but also to help her with her insecurities where her marriage was concerned. She and Porter were getting along so well that Lynn wanted to help Jade keep the relationship intact and not allow any of the insecurities that they both lived with to interfere with her marriage. They were both often reminded of how they could ruin relationships without even trying.

"Yes, Ms. Baxter. I mean, Mrs. Grey." Brooke just couldn't get used to calling Jade by her married name. It was probably because Jade herself couldn't get used to it either. "Yes, I did make an appointment for you. I'll bring in Ms. Walters." Brooke ushered in the journalist who had scheduled the interview with Jade. Her magazine was doing a spread on her, and today would be the beginning of the interview.

The young woman extended her hand towards Jade. "I'm Sandra Walters from Washington Daily, but you can call me Sandi." After she had noticed that Jade was not going to return the courtesy, she eased her hand down to her side as she looked Jade straight into the eye. The journalist could tell this interview was not going to be easy. She remained standing, clenching her iPad.

Jade was her usual, direct, to-the-point self. "Hi, have a seat there," she said, pointing to the purple, Italian leather chair situated directly in front of her desk. "I'm sure you know that I only agreed to *one* hour, correct?" she added bluntly, pointing and nodding at the same time.

"Yes, Ms. Baxter, or is it Mrs. Grey? I was told that you were recently married."

Jade looked at her with very inquisitive eyes, trying to figure out where exactly this young woman was coming from, careful not to reveal too much. "Ms. Baxter is fine," Jade chided as she sat down next to the journalist in a matching chair. Jade's office was ultra-contemporary. African American art created by some of the most famous artists of the century filled the room. Color was showcased in every aspect of the décor. It was evident that everything had been personally hand selected. No off-the-shelf furniture for Jade.

Jade looked down at her watch. "So let's get started!"

Sandi had been told to get Jade to talk about her new campaign, "Own Your Truth," and to get as much dirt as she could on her as to what exactly initiated the whole thing. People were still curious about the details of the event that happened between Jade and Lynn last year.

"Ms. Baxter," Sandi started, "tell me about your Own Your Truth campaign. How did you come up with that name? How's it going? Oh, and before you begin, do you mind if I record you?"

"No, not at all." Jade crossed her legs and eased back in the chair, exuding the confidence that had gotten her to this point of commanding interviews for major magazines and newspapers. "There comes a time in life when you realize that you may not be living your true life or being your true self. You're in denial. You're living up to other people's expectations of you."

"I see," said Sandi. "So you just decided to create this campaign to help you find the real you?"

Jade looked at her very cautiously, knowing that she did not want to reveal too much and that these journalists would take any little thing that people said and run with it to sell their product. She had to choose her words carefully. "Not so much me, but I wanted to help others to realize their true potential. The truth is empowering."

"Okay, so you're really about empowering people?" Sandi asked as she slowly eased into her next question. "Like the incident with your sister last year?"

Jade was not surprised by the question. She knew it was coming; it was just a matter of when. "Yes,

Sandi. It was that incident with my sister that made me realize that I needed to come clean about some things in my life that I had been hiding for years. I decided that I wanted to help other women discover their inner beauty and know that it is okay to have a past, and if they embrace those truths and move on, life will be so much more fulfilling."

Sandi wanted Jade to talk more about what was so compelling in her personal life, especially some of those things that Lynn had blurted out at the conference. She tried another angle. "Ms. Baxter, how do you feel about the most recent legislation passed in Colorado for legal use of marijuana?"

Jade sat up in the chair and crossed her hands over her knees. "Sandi, because I have done some pretty unacceptable things in my life, I have no room to judge people. There was a period in my life where I experimented with drugs, and I can rightfully thank the type of people that I allowed being in my life at that time for that. Yes, I take total responsibility for my very blemished past, but I've learned so much from my experiences and those people from my past that I want to encourage and inspire other women to accept themselves for who they are." Jade looked down at her watch and was glad that the time was passing fast. She could tell that this young journalist was trying to scoop up some juicy gossip on her to make her article sizzle, and sell some magazines.

Before the journalist could ask the next question, Brooke opened the door, stuck her head in, and said, "Mrs. Grey, Addie's school just called. They are having some issues and would like for you to give them a call right away."

Jade jumped up from the chair. "Okay, thank you, Brooke. Sandi, would you please excuse me? I need to deal with this; as a matter of fact, can we just finish this another day? Let my assistant know that I said it is okay for you to reschedule."

Sandi looked very disappointed, not so much at the fact that Jade was kicking her out but at not knowing what was so important that Jade felt that she had to deal with it right now. Could it be something that would have fit just fine in the interview? Nonetheless, she knew she had to go. So be it.

As Sandi exited the office, Jade dialed the school on her iPhone. "Yes, this is Jade Baxter Grey, Addie Grey's mom. I was asked to give you a call, is she okay?" Jade was getting used to identifying herself as Addie's mom. She and Porter had decided that stepmother was cold and distant.

The tone of the voice on the other end let Jade know that Addie had been acting up again. This had become a way of life ever since she had begun helping Porter with Addie. Addie was four years old now, and she was beginning to get a little jealous of their relationship. Porter paid more than enough attention to her, and so did Jade for that matter; however, Addie had started missing her mother more and more as she grew older. "Well, Mrs. Grey, actually, Addie is physically okay, but emotionally we think that she might need some counseling. Are you and her father available for a conference soon?" the principal asked.

Jade could tell they meant business at the school, so she knew she had better say something to let them know that she and Porter were very supportive of Addie and the school. "Yes, sure, I'll check with her father to see when he can meet with you either this week or one day next. In the meantime, I'll come right over to get her."

This was not something that Jade needed at this point in her life, but she knew when she married Porter that she agreed to accept the responsibility of raising Addie. She was such a pretty little girl and super smart. Her features strikingly resembled her mother's. Jade just couldn't figure out why her behavior could be so obnoxious at times. *Oh, well,* she thought to herself, *we'll just have to deal with it.* With that, she hurriedly put her papers away and started to clean her desk.

On her way out, she stopped at Brooke's desk. "Brooke? When is my appointment with the psychiatrist?" She was feeling the need more and more now to see him.

"Actually, Ms. Baxter, I was gonna let you know that it is for next Monday at 9:30 a.m. Your schedule was clear for then. Is that day and time still gonna work for you?"

"Yes, that will be fine, Brooke. Thank you so much, and cancel everything for the rest of the day. Thanks!"

Chapter 5

Lynn

Lynn continued to see Dr. Hamilton after the incident with her sister, Jade. She loved the visits, actually, and she saw some benefits from the sessions. Today was one of those days. It made her heart happy to know that Jade was going to start seeing him as well. They had come a long way; however, they both had a long way to go individually and together, as sisters and as a family.

"Morning, Ms. Baxter!" Dr. Hamilton greeted her.

The handshakes had turned into hugs over time— not the kind that Lynn would have preferred, but just being able to get close to him to touch and smell him was enough to keep her coming back. "Morning,

Doc!"

"How are things between you and Jade?" he asked.

"Well, doctor, we are doing so much better. I am not her problem anymore. It's her stepdaughter, Addie, who has her wrapped up now. I'm sure that she will share some of that with you when she sees you next Monday."

"Okay and how are you these days?" he asked as if he knew that there had been something troubling her.

"I just keep having these recurring dreams about Gabe."

Dr. Hamilton asked what the dreams were about, and she told him that all she could see was his face and, on occasion, what the plane must have looked like when it crashed. He explained to her that it was normal for a wife to experience this after suddenly losing her husband.

He felt that she had not ever really dealt with Gabe's death because of her situation with Jade and her relationship with Casey. "How are things with you and Casey?"

That brought a smile to her face as she answered. "Casey and I are fine. Actually, we may be getting married soon."

Dr. Hamilton seemed somewhat surprised. "Really now, that serious?"

"Yeah, we've been talking about it, even looked at some rings."

"Is there any hesitancy on your part, Lynn?"

Lynn thought to herself that either she must have been coming here too much, or he had truly figured out her modus operandi. "To be honest, doctor…yes, there is. I'm not really sure what's going on, but I do know that I love Casey. I am going to marry him."

She relaxed on the comfortable sofa as she had done for over a year now. She couldn't believe what she had done to bring her to Dr. Hamilton in the first place, nor could she believe her initial reluctance in agreeing to follow through on her appointments with him. Lynn was ashamed of the prank she had pulled on Jade last year, but the results of it far outweighed the crime. Now, Lynn had fallen in love with the idea of coming to see her psychiatrist.

There had been light moments and dark moments spent on this couch, in this room, with this doctor, and oh, what a fine doctor he was. Fine as in handsome. Dr. Hamilton had a smooth, suave way of making you dig real deep down in your soul to relieve you of any layers of dirt that may be buried within, and today was no different.

He smiled that million-dollar smile, showing all

thirty-two of those pearly white teeth of his. These were times when Lynn really felt comfortable and relaxed in his presence.

There were also times when she got the urge to just forget all protocol and who they were and snatch him down on top of her on that expensive leather sofa. Many days she fantasized about the two of them touching and kissing while she relieved him of that Brooks Brothers suit and that Zegna white, textured shirt. She figured he shopped at either Neiman's or Bergdorf's. She knew these clothes because sometimes she would accompany Jade when she would shop for Porter. Lynn was always mesmerized and almost in a trance when the aroma of his Tom Ford Venetian Bergamot Eau de Parfum wafted into her nose and straight to her brain. That scent lingered long after the doctor visits were over.

They finished their session, and Lynn went home to prepare dinner for herself and Casey. The drive home gave her some time to think about him, and she decided what she was going to do.

Chapter 6

Jade

"Hello, Porter? How's your day going?" Jade could tell that Porter was having a trying day by the way he answered the phone. She hated to hit him with the news about Addie, but she wanted to do it in the car as opposed to when they all got home around the dinner table.

"Hey, babe! It's been crazy busy today, can't wait to get home and just squeeze you."

Jade didn't want to give him the bad news in the midst of the warmness she was feeling from him at that moment but knew she had to. "Yeah, baby, I feel the same way, but we'll have to deal with Addie first."

"Oh, no, what is it this time? Did the school call again? Why didn't they call me?" he questioned angrily.

"Yes, they did, not sure if they tried to get you or not, but they want us to come down for a conference. See what day you are free, and I'll take it from there," she assured him. Jade knew Porter liked for her to take ownership when it came to Addie. He was no fool either and knew that the way Addie was conceived was nothing that he wanted rehashed with Jade. He felt very proud that Jade had accepted her and loved her like her own despite the fact that affair he'd had with Addie's mother four years ago, never *ever* went away. Although Jade never threw it in his face after Addison's death delivering Addie; Porter knew that his brief affair with Addison was always there in the back of Jade's mind. He thought of Addison often when he looked at Addie, who was named after her mother.

He glanced at his iPhone quickly and said, "I can do Monday."

Jade was about to say yes until it dawned on her that she had already made the psych appointment for Monday, and she did not want to miss it. "I have a doctor's appointment on Monday Porter, and I won't be able to make it."

"Doctor's appointment? Are you okay?" he asked her with concern.

"Yes, Porter, I'm fine. Remember I told you that I was going to go and check out that therapist Lynn is seeing?" She was careful not to use the word psychiatrist because she didn't want to frighten him. "Can you do Tuesday? I can check with the school when I get there to see if they can meet then."

"Yeah, that'll work. Damn! I don't know what's gotten into that girl. I'll see you guys at home later on, okay? Love you!"

Jade always loved to hear him say "I love you" at the end of every call.

As the driver pulled up to the school, she could see Addie outside waiting with her friends and teacher. She was such a beautiful little girl, but she looked so much like her mother that it was a wonder that Jade wasn't the one with issues. So many times Jade had had nightmares about Addison and Porter being together when she and Porter would have their little spats and breakups, but she refused to bring it up with him now. She knew that most of those thoughts were coming from her insecurities and problems committing and trusting in relationships. Besides Addison was gone, and now it was just the two of them, plus one.

"Come on, Addie, hop in! Hi, Marissa! Do you want me to sign her out?" Jade had decided to just call the school to set up the meeting instead of going in. She was a bit tired and didn't want to be bothered with all of the drama today. The driver opened the door for Addie as she crawled in beside Jade.

"That's okay Ms. Grey. I'll sign her out for you. See you tomorrow, Addie," Marissa said as she helped Addie into the car.

"Hey, Addie girl! How was your day today?" Jade asked as she reached over to give her a kiss.

Addie pulled away. "It was okay."

Jade could tell that she was not her usual self. "Did anything happen in school today, Addie?"

"No" was her response as she frowned and crossed her little arms over her chest, pouting a little. She was dressed so cutely in her pink wool jacket. Those jeans fit her perfectly like her mother's used to. Each morning was a challenge with her full head of hair. Addie always wanted to wear it down, but Jade insisted that she wear it in braids or ponytails with some kind of ribbon, barrette, or headband. She liked for her to look like a little girl. Her sneakers were glittery silver with wide shoe strings. All the girls her age wore those type of shoes.

"Addie? The school called me at work today, and they want to talk with your father and me. They said you've been acting out. What did you do today?"

Addie paused for a long while as if she were trying to think of the right words to say. What she was about to say would have been hard for any grown up, especially to your stepmother. "Well, I really miss my mommy, and I wish she were here with me instead of you!"

At that moment, Jade felt torn. On one hand, she empathized with little Addie about never having known her mother, but on the other hand, it angered her that Porter had had an affair with her mother. Not to mention how much of a struggle it had been for her personally to step up and act as a surrogate mother when she didn't even have kids of her own. She wasn't quite sure how to handle this situation.

Porter had cared for her alone the first three years of her life and never hid the fact from Addie that her mother had died. He always told her in a way that she could understand that her mommy was in heaven and that one day they would all be together again. Jade wondered where she would fit into that picture now that they were married and one big happy family.

"Come here, Addie," she said. Addie laid her head on Jade's lap. Jade stroked her back and her hair, offering her words of encouragement. "Addie, I know you miss your mommy, but remember what your daddy tells you?"

"About what?" Addie answered without even looking up.

Jade was searching for words that she hoped

would comfort her. "Remember how he says that one day you'll see your mommy again?"

Addie started to cry. "I know, but I want to see her now."

Jade was glad that they were just about to pull into the driveway, and thank goodness Porter had made it home before them. As the driver parked the car, Porter walked out to meet them.

He opened the door on the passenger side where Addie was sitting. "Hey there, baby girl!" he greeted as he began to unbuckle her seat belt. He immediately saw the tears. "What's wrong? Why are you crying?" He looked over at Jade as he lifted Addie out of the car and hugged her.

She laid her head on his shoulder and cried. "I miss my mommy, and I want to see her now."

Porter looked so sad as if he didn't quite know what to say. By this time, Jade had already gotten out the car and the driver was helping her with Addie's book bag and things. Porter had totally forgotten to speak to Jade; this happened a lot when Addie was in one of her "I miss my mommy" moods.

They all walked into the house and Porter sat down with Addie. Sometimes Jade wondered if this sad, "I miss my mommy" attitude, was all an act on Addie's part when she knew she was in trouble at school. She let Porter deal with it and decided that she would have a bath before dinner.

In her heart, she was hoping that she could stay strong and not ever let her emotions get the best of her where Addie was concerned because she was just a little girl. She loved Porter, and that was the most important thing.

Chapter 7

Casey and Lynn

Three months later

"Hey Lynn, whatcha' doing this week?" Casey asked Lynn over the phone.

"I don't know, a little work over the weekend. Why're you asking?"

"How about we get a couple of plane tickets and fly to Las Vegas or Mexico?"

"What? Have you lost your mind?" Lynn laughed.

"No," Casey answered in a very matter of fact tone.

"Just up and go to Vegas or leave the country in

the middle of the week?" Lynn sat down at her desk. "Okay, any particular reason we should just up and go like this?"

"Sure it is!" he said with excitement. "We need to get married."

"What? Are you serious, Casey? Really? You're ready to get married?"

"I've been thinkin', why keep putting it off? We're going to be together forever. I love you, Lynn."

"Oh Casey, I love you too. I was going to ask you if you wanted to buy tickets to see Teena Marie Thursday night at the Birchmere. Looks like I'll be buying plane tickets instead."

"So I take it that's a yes? You'll marry me?" he asked.

"You're so silly. Of course, I'll marry you!" she said giggling.

"Well then why don't you get tickets, you pick the place, and we'll discuss the details when I get there this evening. Love you, Lynn."

Tears began to stream down Lynn's face as she clicked off her cell phone, held it tightly in her hands, and leaned back in her chair. Was it true? Did she really say yes to another marriage proposal? Was she ready to remarry, especially since she still had recurring memories and dreams about Gabe? Her next thought was to call Jade to share her good news. A little reluctant for several reasons, she decided to wait. She knew that her twin sister was going through a lot with Porter and Addie. Lynn did not want to hear Jade rain on her parade or plant any more doubts in her mind about Casey. Jade always had been jealous of her happiness with men. Neither one of them was batting a thousand, she thought to herself.

Immediately, Lynn turned on her computer and started a Google search for the tickets to Mexico. "Yes!" she said under her breath, pleased with the first ad result "Hmmm…romantic vacations in Mexico." Lynn stopped for a minute to answer her cell phone thinking Casey was calling her right back.

"Hey, baby! I'm searching…" Hearing silence on the other end, she quickly said, "Hello, hello. Anybody there? Who is this?"

Not a word. This was beginning to annoy Lynn. Her next thought was to change her number, but that would be such a major inconvenience for her that she totally said no to the thought.

She went back to her computer and decided on Cancun, Mexico as their destination wedding vacation. The tickets weren't too expensive, and they could leave as early as Saturday. She couldn't believe it. In about four days, she would be Mrs. Casey Carter. Now what to pack? Shopping at Victoria's Secret was a must on the list before she packed.

Chapter 8

Dr. Joseph E. Hamilton

"Dr. Hamilton, your eight o 'clock appointment is here."

"Thank you, Ms. Shaw. Have the nurse bring him in."

Dr. Joseph E. Hamilton, one of the most renowned psychiatrists in the world, had offices in the District, Maryland, and Virginia—better known as the DMV. Patients would spend their last dime to see him. The stigma society placed on mental health had not hurt his business one bit. One visit to his office and the patients were hooked. Unlike Lynn and Jade Baxter, some people had serious issues, and Dr. Hamilton had a manner about him that made them feel so comfortable that they would spill every problem they had and hoped that he couldn't solve them for many visits. Each patient felt special when in his care. He just had an air of confidence, and he was calm and down to earth, unlike many other doctors who lacked good bedside manners.

Women from all walks of life filled his office daily. He was known to handle a lot of domestic violence victims pro bono. He also served on the boards of organizations and shelters that dealt with women and children who were victims of or impacted by abuse. He cared so much that some wondered if he may have had some experience in that arena himself.

No novice to media recognition and peer accolades, he was truly an advocate for people suffering from mental illness and he was very popular. He had chosen not to marry as of yet, and as far as the world knew, he had no children. It certainly wasn't for lack of availability nor was it his personal profile.

Materially, it was obvious that he had many paying patients. His outward appearance spoke of a man who was mild mannered and did good deeds for the underserved.

On many occasions, patients were referred to him when all hope was lost. Today was no different. A referral from his old Meharry Med School buddy was about to challenge him once again.

Last week, he had seen one of his college buddies, Dr. Mohammed Abdul, at a conference in Atlanta. His friend had moved there and set up his practice after graduation. They talked extensively about how well each other's businesses were going. Mohammed was seeing a patient who was in an unusual situation.

"Hey, Joe," Mohammed had said. "I have a patient that could benefit from seeing you. Got any time when you get back to D.C.? I know for a fact that he will be there next week taking care of some business. Could you talk to him for a few minutes, and then you and I can discuss your observations?"

Curious as to why Mohammed couldn't help him, Joe asked, "You can't help him?" Joe knew that Mohammed was a psychiatrist, and in the past few years, he had targeted his practice more to adolescent patients living on the Autism spectrum.

They both smiled and shook their heads at the same time.

"Nah, man, I've been seeing him for over six months now, and he could use someone like you who has more experiences than I do in adult mental health issues. Besides, everybody knows you're Dr. Joe Hamilton, best in the world!"

Joe got up to leave, bumping fists with Mohammed. "Have him call me!"

That was how he was. He never knew how to say no.

Tapping lightly on the door, Ms. Shaw ushered in the new patient. "Come on in, have a seat." Dr. Hamilton extended his hand to him. "Dr. Joe Hamilton."

"Alexander Kenneth Adams. Pleased to meet you," he responded, offering a firm handshake in return. "And thank you for seeing me on such short notice."

Dr. Hamilton straightened his necktie as they both sat down. Necktie straightening seemed to be a habitual thing with him. He always touched his tie at the knot, straightened it, and held it in place as he sat. It wasn't clear if he worried about a straight tie or if he wanted to showcase his Rolex rose gold watch or his diamond ring, worn on his right pinky finger. He was left handed.

"So, Mr. Adams—"

"Alex, please."

Dr. Hamilton was happy to oblige him on the first name. He had learned that patients seemed to feel calmer when he called them by their first name; however, he kept the patient-doctor relationship strictly professional. At all times, he was Dr. Hamilton.

"Alex, what brings you to D.C.? Even more so, what brings you in to see me?" Joe Hamilton leaned back in his black leather high-back chair, as he rested both hands on the armrests and rested his right ankle on his left knee, giving Alex full view of those brown gator shoes he was wearing. "I have reviewed most of your files that Dr. Abdul faxed over to me. How can I help you? "While Alex was speaking, Joe Hamilton took a moment to observe the man sitting in front of him. What he saw was a relaxed man very casually dressed in khaki slacks and a body-fitting black turtleneck cashmere sweater that allowed his toned muscles to peek through each time he moved. He was wearing black loafer like shoes. His six foot and then some body frame boasted of a daily exercise regimen. Joe had already peeped Alex's vitals on his chart from the nurse, so he knew that he was in his late forties, though he didn't look a day over thirty. His hair was cut short but not close. His skin was in hues of brown and very tight. It looked as though he had had some plastic surgery done on his face. He appeared very confident as he spoke. Joe noticed that Alex used his hands a lot to express his thoughts.

"Well, as you can see from reading my chart, I have a very serious case of memory loss, which makes it hard for me to hold down a job. I am here this week in hopes of landing a job in D.C., something that will be routine and will not take a lot of skills and training. I have almost no recollection of who I used to be or what I used to do professionally before my accident."

"Do you remember where you're from, Alex?" Joe had many questions but felt that he should take it slow, sensing that Alex may be a little hesitant to reveal a lot on the first visit. The number one question that he wanted an answer to was what had happened to put him in the coma he read about in his file.

"I remember that I'm originally from Atlanta and that I have no family. They tell me I was in a tragic car accident, and my car was totaled. I was in a medically induced coma for about five months because of the trauma and impact to my head during the accident. After my hospital stay and recovery, I was released and started seeing Dr. Abdul for therapy. "Alex went on to explain to Joe that he had made considerable progress after he had come out of the coma, and he knew Dr. Abdul was a major part of that success, as well as the nurse who had cared for him. This nurse, Halle, actually volunteered to take him home when she found out his story and that he had no family. She took splendid care of him for months and had begun to have feelings for him. He was very grateful to her, but he had always sensed that there may be more to his life's story than what he was witnessing at that time. Nurse Halle was the one who had filled him in about the accident. He told Dr. Hamilton that he decided it was best for him to move for a fresh start, and if he moved to D.C., he wanted to make sure he continued his therapy as not to impede the progress made so far in regaining his memory. Nurse Halle was heartbroken when she heard the news that he was moving and made him promise to keep in touch and let her know his whereabouts. Halle had fallen for him hard, so much so that when she realized that he might one day leave, she began saving money to help him on his initial journey. Part of her did not want to tell him this, but she knew she had to because he was so determined to leave. She prayed that he would keep in contact with her and that they would meet again. Dr. Hamilton told him that he would be more than happy to take him on as a patient, but he could not guarantee him miraculous results from their future sessions. Alex got up to leave, firmly shaking Joe's hand and assuring him that he did not expect any miracles because being alive was all the miracle that he needed. Joe told him to make an appointment for next week and wished him well on his job search.

Chapter 9

Casey and Lynn

"Ladies and gentleman, the captain has turned on the fasten seat belt signs. Please return all tray tables to their upright positions," the flight attendant directed the passengers.

Casey and Lynn had slept during the flight, which gave them plenty of time to nuzzle and be close. They were ready. Casey had gotten the marriage license, and Lynn had made the appointment and reservations with the hotel for the ceremony to take place that night of their arrival. She wanted to spend this trip as Mrs. Carter.

The hotel was only thirty minutes from the airport. Lynn had arranged for limo service to the hotel. When they arrived and secured their luggage at the baggage claim area, they noticed the driver holding the sign with their name, Carter, printed on it. Why not? In a few hours she too would be officially a Carter.

Lynn and Casey had a light dinner in the room and a quick moment on the beautiful, comforted king sized bed before they began to dress for the ceremony. Pulling her close to him and brushing her hair back from her face with his hands, he kissed her with passion. "I love you, Lynn and I'm so glad that you are in my life!" he whispered in her ear.

"I love you too Casey, and I know that we are going to be so happy. I can't wait to say those words, 'I do.' Her favorite place was lying under his arm, with both his arms wrapped around her. This time, she needed to take a minute to think about what she was about to do, and she did not want Casey to see her face. She was afraid that he might detect some sort of hesitancy from her. Her mind traveled back down memory lane to the day that she and Gabe had met and then married. Today was bittersweet; however, she knew that she had prayed for it many nights. She could not deny that she had been so happy with Casey. They had been almost inseparable since Jade's wedding.

About thirty minutes had passed and breaking the silence, Casey nudged her, "Hey, we better get going if we want to make that wedding!"

"*That* wedding? Lynn questioned as she sat up and hit the floor before he did. "That wedding is ours, and I'll race you to the shower!"

About an hour and a half later, they were dressed and waiting in the lobby. People were looking at them and smiling. It was as if they knew what they were about to do. Lynn smiled back proudly.

The ceremony was to be held on the beach property of the hotel. Lynn had ordered an arrangement of red roses with lots of greenery and baby's breath sprinkled in between. She knew that they would look gorgeous against her white cotton two pieced pants suit. The red, wide brim, floppy hat with the white band accented the total ensemble. Her arms were pretty toned for a woman of her age, so the sleeveless top with the deep v-line neck was very sexy. Lynn had found a pair of red patent leather sandals with a small heel that was perfect for the walk from the hotel to the beach. She accessorized her jewelry all in red. The small red drawstring purse she carried on her arms was barely noticeable under the bouquet of flowers.

They held hands as they stopped at the concierge desk to wait for the escort to the beach.

"You look so handsome!" Jade said to Casey as she tiptoed to give him a quick kiss. Though he wasn't too tall, she still needed to reach up just a little to touch his lips when he wasn't the one bending down and initiating the kiss. Casey looked very much in charge in his white outfit. He didn't need a tan because he was born with one. There was no bottle of Banana Boat that could match his complexion. You could almost count the abs through that white body fitting long sleeved shirt. His pants fit him almost as if they had been tailor made. The nude toned sandals were a perfect match for the outfit. His sparkling white teeth set off a smile that out shone the stars in the sky.

"Hello, Mr. and Mrs. Carter?" the gentleman asked as he approached Casey and Lynn and extended his hand.

Both giggling almost in unison. "Not yet!" Casey and Lynn replied.

"Oh, I'm so sorry you're right, not yet!" he laughed with them. "Follow me, please." They followed him through the doors of the hotel onto the beach towards a white gazebo. Lynn grabbed Casey's arms like a young school girl. She was so ecstatic.

As they approached the gazebo, they could see a few other people gathered with clipboards, her bouquet, and a chaplain holding a bible. The sun was just about to set over the calm ocean. There was a light breeze in the air, enough for the palm trees to sway. The company had set up a few white chairs, in the event random beach goers would like to sit and observe. Lynn had agreed to this option.

After greetings and hugs, the chaplain performed the ceremony.

"…and now I pronounce you Mr. and Mrs. Casey Carter. You may kiss the bride!" the chaplain shouted. Everyone around the beach clapped and cheered. They kissed for a long time before releasing each other. There was a waiter passing around champagne to them and a few others who had stopped and witnessed the ceremony. They proposed everlasting toasts to each other. Thanked the wedding planners and strolled along the beach before retiring for their first night as Mr. and Mrs. Casey Carter. Lynn had totally forgotten all about her sister Jade and everything else for that matter.

She would fill her in with all the details when she returned home in a few days.

Chapter 10

Jade and Dr. Hamilton

"No, please stop! Don't kill her!" Jade was crying and screaming. "Stop it! Stop it! Please, stop it!"

Dr. Hamilton handed her a box of Kleenex and tried to comfort her as she once again attempted to delve into the stories of her childhood that had begun to haunt her as an adult.

She sat up, wiped her eyes, blew her nose, and looked Dr. Hamilton in the eyes. "Why does this still hurt so much after all these years?" she asked him.

"Well, Jade, that's the way domestic violence is. The impact can linger for years. You're scarred, but you're healing. The sad thing is that the impact of domestic violence on children is devastating. It does not matter how old that child is. It rears its ugly head in so many different scenarios."

She sniffled and wiped more tears.

"Do you need a break or are you okay with continuing?"

"I want to continue," she said softly.

"Okay, what did you do when you saw your father holding the gun to your mother's head?"

Jade released a huge sigh. "Well, when I got to the bottom of the stairs, he yelled at me to go back to my room. I can still see him holding his arm around her neck with the gun pointed at her head and telling her, 'Bitch, I'll kill you. Don't you know that!?' She was so helpless. I wanted to do something to help her, but I couldn't. "Jade continued to cry, and Dr. Hamilton handed her another handful of tissues as he continued to gently question her. "Jade, do you feel like it was your fault that your father treated your mother that way?"

"Yes," she admitted, wiping her eyes. At this point, she just wanted to pour her heart out and tell him that everything that happened to her mother was all her fault because she had been such a troublemaker growing up.

Dr. Hamilton interrupted her thoughts with, "Talk

about it, Jade."

She wasn't sure if she really could talk about it even though she wanted to. It was hard to believe that she had actually even gotten to the point in her life where she could say anything about her past. She thought that future sessions like this with Dr. Hamilton would be very good for her. "Dr. Hamilton, why do you think this is all bothering me now after all of these years?"

"Well, Jade, there could be a number of reasons. I really don't think we should focus so much on the 'why's' at this point as we should clearing your head and heart. If you'd like to stop here for today and make your appointment for next month, that will be fine. I can tell this is really emotionally draining for you."

Jade sat up and looked at him. She wasn't sure if he was concerned about her or if her story was too much for him on one day. Feeling the need to talk, she began to pour her heart out again. "Okay, um…I was a victim of rape when I was about twelve years old, and I never told anyone because I felt that I had brought the situation upon myself. For the past year or so, I've been having these recurring nightmares about that day and what actually happened. There were three young teen boys who were hiding in another room. I had agreed to skip school that day with one of them. I allowed him to have sex with me, and he allowed the others to follow. As I reflect, I was enamored with the older boy, but never was engaged mentally or physically with the act of sex. How could I be? I was only twelve. It was like a means to an end to just have his attention and the fake act of liking me."

"How did that make you feel, Jade? It sounds as though you had very low self-esteem at that time, and maybe needing more attention and love from your father?" By now, Dr. Hamilton had loosened his necktie, crossed his legs, and leaned back in his chair. "This older boy perhaps supplied that need for you," he said.

Jade continued talking. She laid back on the chaise, closed her eyes, and folded her hands on her stomach. Going back to that day was terrifying, but she wanted to finally talk with someone about it. "Well, Dr. Hamilton, I felt violated. It happened early in the morning, which made it really bad because that meant I had to carry it around with me the rest of the day, and since I'd skipped school, I had nowhere to be. I could not go home because I was supposed to be at school; I could not roam around the neighborhood for fear that the neighbors would see me. The older boy whom I had agreed to have sex with someone that I loved very much, and it was so hurtful that he would do something like that to me, that he would betray me. Somehow it was almost more hurtful than being raped by the other two boys. And he just left, left me there by myself like I was nothing. I knew I had to leave even if I had nowhere to go, and chance a neighbor seeing me and telling my parents later. So I left the apartment he had taken me to and roamed the streets of that neighborhood for hours until it was time for my bus to come. Once the bus arrived all the children got off, laughing, playing and talking about all the innocent things that had happened at school that day. I walked ahead of the crowd, not wanting to face anyone, not having any happy stories to report for the day, not feeling a part of that age group anymore. Ashamed is what I felt." she paused for a moment as if to catch her breath. Dr. Hamilton sat quietly, rested his face in his hand, with his elbow on the chair. Jade started again as she glanced up at the clock on the wall. She could see that her hour was just about up, but she felt that she had so much more to get out.

"Dr. Hamilton at twelve, it was very devastating. I was still a baby, really, and I couldn't process what had happened. I cried all day and cried myself to sleep that night. Strangely enough, when I think about it now, I still cry myself to sleep."

"So, Jade, as traumatic as this whole situation must have been for you and your family, and even now for you to still be thinking about it, how does this relate to the way that your father treated your mother?" he quizzed.

"No, there was so much more that happened, but it was all related to this same boy. By the time I was thirteen, I was pregnant, and this put my family in total discord. My father blamed my mother, and my mother blamed my father." Jade began to cry again. They both blamed each other for being failures as parents.

Dr. Hamilton waited. Not one word from him as he let her regroup and start again.

"My mother and father were so hurt by this that my mother literally lost her mind. One day she was so distraught with everything that my father had to call 911 because she had undressed and run outside of our home naked and crawled up a tree in our yard. There she sat, crying, shivering, and holding on to a branch. The ambulance came, and they put her in a strait jacket and hauled her off to a mental institution. I will never forget the look on her face. I saw that look once more in her lifetime, and that was the night that we had her taken away to a hospice facility. It was a look of disbelief and helplessness." Jade turned her body over to the side and raised her knees up to her chest in a fetal position. She did not look at Dr. Hamilton. Instead she looked down and let the tears roll.

"These things, Dr. Hamilton, have weighed heavily on my heart and mind for years, but I have managed to push them away up until now. I had always blamed myself and felt guilt whenever there was confusion in our home. It is all so strange that these memories are resurfacing this late in my life. I believe my relationships have all been hurt because of these deep feelings.

"Jade you should not feel guilty. You are not to blame. You and your siblings were victims as much as your mother was." Dr. Hamilton said.

"Watching my father constantly physically abuse my mother was not easy. I vowed that I would never let a man treat me that way; however, throughout the years, I must have forgotten that vow because there were so many times that I let physical and verbal abuse lurk into my relationships. I just went along to get along. It was almost like I accepted it as normal behavior between a man and a woman." Jade sat up again and then she stood up. "Dr. Hamilton, I think I've talked enough today. I should be going."

He stood up as well, and this time, he actually broke with professionalism and reached out to give Jade a hug. At first, she jerked away as if startled that he was actually trying to touch her. Then she accepted the welcoming hug, and the tears flowed down her cheeks.

"I'll see you next month?" he asked her, then added, "Look, why don't I leave and you just sit here for a while until you pull yourself together?"

She picked up her purse and nodded yes as she paused before sitting back down. "Okay, thanks, Dr. Hamilton. I think I will." She watched him walk out of the door.

When Jade finally left, the receptionist stared at her as if she had heard every word. "See you next month, Ms. Baxter?" she asked very solemnly.

"Yes, same date and time will work for me. Thanks."

Chapter 11

Alex

Alex landed a job at a large not-for-profit organization in the District. So far they were the only ones who were willing to take a chance with him and his sketchy background. His job was to assist the executive director with any tasks that were needed. He found an affordable studio apartment which meant that he could now move the rest of his things to Washington, D.C., which wasn't that much. The most important thing was that he would now be able to continue seeing Dr. Joe Hamilton on a regular basis. He was so excited that he decided to celebrate by treating himself to Starbucks.

Walking down K Street, he could spot Starbucks a block away. Wrapped up in a black double-breasted pea coat with a gray and black skull cap pulled way down over his ears, you could barely see those naturally manicured eyebrows of his, but his straight pointy nose and thin curved lips were very prominent. He had high cheeks and firm jaw bones. Black leather driving gloves covered his hands. Alex was prepared for the fickle weather in this town. March was feeling like January. D.C. was an interesting place to live. Almost like Hollywood, you never knew who you would meet on the streets of D.C. In the mornings and at lunch, the streets and nearby shops were always filled with people who were famous in their own rights, like judges, politicians, and congressmen and women. On rare occasions, POTUS was known to step out of the White House and visit some of the shops.

The line of people going in and out of the door was a dead giveaway that he was in downtown D.C. "Mocha whip, please," he said to the barista, and then he turned to the woman standing in line next to him and said, "Busy place, huh?"

"Yes, it's always like this, twenty-four seven," she answered back. "Vanilla Latte," she said walking closer to the counter.

Alex began to walk towards the pickup area. Not far behind was the woman, trying to find her space with all of the others who were waiting for their drinks. "Come here often?" he asked her.

"Actually, I'm in here twice a day sometimes." She smiled back at him. Out of all of the people who were in the place, it was odd that he would single her out to talk to.

"I'm Alex Adams, and you are?" He extended his gloved hand.

Reaching for his hand, she replied, "I'm Lynn Baxter."

He smiled at her and couldn't take his eyes away from hers. It was almost like he had met her at another time, but he knew that that could not be the case because, of course, he was new to D.C.

Lynn was bundled in her tan cashmere long coat with her favorite brown hounds tooth scarf tied neatly around her neck. The brown leather knee high boots were popping under that coat.

"Mocha whip for Alex!" the barista yelled.

Alex excused himself and walked over to the counter to get his drink. Before he left, he felt that he had to say one more thing to her. "Hope to see you in here again,"

Lynn smiled back and just nodded her head in agreement, as her drink order was up next.

Chapter 12

Lynn and Alex

Weeks had passed, and Casey seemed to be working more and more at night. Lynn was beginning to feel neglected. She began to look forward to her Starbucks meetings with Alex. The meetings had no longer become coincidental. It did not help that she had given him her cell phone number, and they were beginning to talk quite often.

Today, Starbucks seemed more crowded than usual. The line to order was super long, but no one seemed to care because they knew what would be waiting at the end of the line. An irresistible drink of choice.

"Vanilla Latte please!" Lynn smiled at the young girl taking the order. She looked very new and excited to be at work. She handed her the exact change and wondered what the young people would do without technology to help them count.

"Vanilla Latte," another voice shouted out behind her. As she turned, she was surprised but happy to see Alex. She was beginning to recognize his gruff voice. Hearing it several times a week now made it easy.

"Hey, Lynn!" Alex moved closer to her as he spoke into her ear. She smiled and leaned closer to him, enjoying all the attention.

"Hey, Alex. What's up? And did I hear you order a Vanilla Latte?" They both walked over to the pickup station after paying.

"Yes, I want what you're having! How about tonight?" Alex asked her.

"Tonight? What about tonight?" she jokingly mocked him.

"You and me, babe. We've been talking for weeks now. I know you're feeling what I'm feeling."

"Vanilla Latte for Lynn and Alex," shouted the barista. They both picked up their coffees and headed towards a table in the corner. Lynn was starting to pay attention to how much time she was spending every day with Alex. Her trips to Starbucks were starting to multiply. She was even paying more attention to what she chose to wear each day proving that she basked in his attention. Her accessories had to complement whatever she was wearing. Big earrings in any style and color were a staple for her. Sometimes she would even layout accessories before she actually chose an outfit to wear. She favored various styles of boots during the cold months. Lynn had taken very good care of herself over the years. It was easy to see how any man would be attracted to her. At five feet five inches, she had maintained her weight so that her wardrobe consisted of no sizes larger than a ten. She loved clothes, and her closets vouched for that need and want. Her beautiful brown hair was always tied back neatly so that she could wear her hats. During the summer, the barber could count on seeing her at least once a month, until August. The short haircut made her look even more youthful. It always grew back fast by the end of the summer and beginning of fall. Each day started out with prayer and meditation and then on to the exercise equipment in the basement of her home. That used to be a ritual with her and Gabe.

"Alex, you know I'm married. What are you talking about feelings for you?" she asked him as if the question was totally absurd.

"I know you're married, but I also know that you gave me your phone number and meet me here every day. Sometimes by the way you talk, it sounds as if you have some doubts about your relationship."

Lynn was not ready for this. How dare him be that factual with her. "Well no, um, no problems with my relationship, Alex," Lynn said in a very firm tone. He was right, though, she thought. Why had she met him here day after day? Why had she given him her cell phone number? She was wondering if some of her insecurities were creeping back. What other reason could it be? Why couldn't she be satisfied in her marriage to Casey?

"Lynn, meet me today after work at the bridge near the Potomac. Just to talk," he pleaded with her. Lynn loved to hear him begging like that, and it wasn't the first time. He really didn't have to beg too long and hard because, for some reason, she was already saying yes. But why?

"Okay, Alex," she agreed. "Around five thirty, but I can't stay long. I have to get home." He had heard her say that on many occasions. Their time together up to this point had been quick sprints in cars, in closed areas inside buildings, and a time or two on the bridge in Virginia. They would kiss and hug and be as intimate as possible careful to not get caught for indecent exposure in public. Lynn knew that this day would come.

A few weeks had passed, and she agreed to meet Alex at a hotel in Virginia. They checked in and cautiously opened the door to the room. It almost seemed as if they both had reservations about what they were doing. Once the door was opened and they were in, Alex slowly took Lynn into his arms, and they kissed passionately. Not like all the kisses in the car and on the bridge and outside of Starbucks. No, there was something different about this kiss. Lynn could feel it deep in her soul.

Alex removed her jacket. "Alex wait!" Lynn stopped. "What are we doing, Alex? What am I doing?" she asked, pulling her jacket back on. He pretended not to hear her and took her jacket off. This time, she helped him. He backed her slowly down on the bed. They acted like two people who had had a relationship for a long time.

Lynn couldn't believe how familiar and safe she felt with him. This stranger. The new man in town. Strangely enough, she didn't even think about the fact that she was married and what it would do to Casey if he ever found out.

She inched her body more on the bed as she watched Alex take off his clothes. At that moment, if someone had asked her to describe his physical appearance, she would have said Denzel Washington's twin. His eyes and hair were as dark as coal against his chocolate brown skin. He had taken care of himself. It was obvious that when he was not calling her or meeting her at Starbucks, he was in somebody's gym.

Before she knew it, Alex had begun undressing

her, and she had no energy to stop him. Her will outweighed her energy. It was only moments until they were immersed into each other and reached the highest level of ecstasy. It was blissful, rapturous, and intense. They were overpowered with emotions. They held each other in a state of great joy before they closed their eyes to reminisce on what had just taken place.

After about an hour, not saying a lot, they both got dressed. The silence between them spoke volumes. Lynn went home to Casey.

Chapter 13

Jade, Porter, and Addie

Jade felt that the weekend had come and gone so fast, and the appointment with Dr. Hamilton didn't help much on Monday. Tuesday was here, and it was time to go to Addie's school. "Come in Mr. and Mrs. Grey." The principal of Addie's school directed them to the nice-looking chairs that appeared to be strategically placed in front of her desk.

"Thank you, Ms. Brown," Porter replied as he pulled one of the chairs away from the desk so that Jade could ease into it.

"We're going to wait just a few minutes more for Addie's teacher if you don't mind," she said.

Porter and Jade sat in their seats, tense and full of

anxiety as to what the principal might tell them about Addie.

It was quiet as Ms. Brown continued to work at her desk. Porter and Jade looked at each other but didn't utter a word. They could read each other very well. After about five minutes, Ms. Aaron walked in looking as frazzled as any Pre-Kindergarten teacher would.

"Hi, I'm Ms. Aaron, Addie's lead teacher."

Ms. Brown spoke up before Jade and Porter could say anything. "Ms. Aaron, this is Mr. and Mrs. Porter Grey."

They all shook hands as she backed into the third seat that was placed on the right-hand side of Porter. The meeting went on for about an hour as they shared all of the behaviors Addie had been exhibiting lately. They came short of suggesting that they have her tested. Of course, by law, they could not suggest that Addie needed to see a psychiatrist, but they came pretty close.

"Addie cries a lot. She appears to be very sensitive lately," the teacher reported. "Is there anything going on at home that we should know about here?"

That's how it is in the schools nowadays, Jade thought. *As soon as a child starts having any problems at school, the first blame is in the home.*

"No, not at all. Addie has everything at home that any young girl would need or want," Jade chimed in.

"And parents and family who love her dearly," Porter added.

"Okay, Mr. and Mrs. Grey," the principal offered, "if I were you, I would take the data that we are giving you today and share it with Addie's pediatrician and see if they can offer you some suggestions for next steps. One thing we cannot and will not tolerate is physical taunting of another student." Ms. Brown stood as if to say, *okay, this meeting is over.* "Please speak with Addie about that and let us know what her doctor says."

Porter and Jade stood from their seats and thanked them both for their time. They reassured the school that they would speak with Addie as well as follow up with her pediatrician. They also guaranteed them that she would not be fighting with the kids anymore. That was a tall order, though, especially since they didn't know exactly why Addie was acting out. The only thing that they could think of was because she was missing her mother.

Porter and Jade exited the building and climbed into their car. The driver was right on time.

"How about lunch, babe? We can talk about this a little more."

Jade didn't really want to talk about it anymore.

Some days she just didn't feel like sharing the burdens that came with parenting. She loved Porter more than anything in her life and Addie too; however, when it came to the issues and problem-solving for Addie, she sometimes just felt like telling Porter that it was his daughter and his problem.

He looked so pitiful and helpless that she could not do that today. "Sure, let's have lunch. Where would you like to go?"

Porter's face and spirit seemed to light up just a little as he instructed the driver to take them to the Palm Restaurant at Tysons. The drive there was short, and the two of them didn't talk much during the ride. He always liked to put his hand on one of her knees. It was almost like a confirmation to her that everything would be okay. Once they arrived, the driver opened the door for Jade as Porter rushed around the car to help her out. "We'll text you when we're ready, Jonas."

"Sure, Mr. G. I'll be close," he said.

The Palm, like The Capital Grille, was filled with people discussing business at lunch time, but the caricatures on the walls at the Palm kept you a little bit more entertained than The Capital Grille while waiting for your meal, and not having a lot to say to the person sitting in front of you. Trying to figure out who was who took your mind off your own problems for a while. And so it was today.

Chapter 14

Dr. Hamilton and Lynn

"Hello, Mrs. Carter. I'm calling from Dr. Hamilton's office to let you know that he'd like for you to come in and meet with him as soon as you possibly can."

"Is there a problem?" Immediately, Lynn wondered if she had been seen somewhere with Alex or if Dr. Hamilton had really analyzed one of their sessions and figured out that she was seeing another man.

"Well, ma'am, he doesn't discuss the why's with us. I just schedule the appointments. Is tomorrow at 10:00 a.m. okay for you?"

"Yes, I think so. Let me check my schedule, and I

will confirm via text. Is Dr. Hamilton available now? I'd like to speak with him."

"No, Ms. Carter, he's with another patient at this time. I will await your text. Take care now!"

Lynn hung up the phone wondering what could be so urgent that Dr. Hamilton had to see her right away. Immediately, her thoughts went to Jade, and she wondered if anything out of the ordinary had happened to her crazy butt. All she could do now was wait the night away until tomorrow.

She thought that maybe she'd give Jade a call to try to feel her out and see if everything seemed okay with her, Porter, and Addie. That way, if it was something related to them, she could prepare herself. Well, maybe, she could never prepare herself for anything where Jade was concerned.

"Hey, girl, what's up?" Lynn asked Jade as she picked up the phone.

"Hey, sis, not much. Just trying to deal with the daily grind and issues popping up here and there with Addie. She is so missing her mom these days. Porter seems to be playing into her little hands. So much so that it's kinda making me sick. I seem to be coming in second these days. Enough about us. What've you been up to?"

"About the same over here. Casey and I are working all the time. We seem to be missing each other a lot lately with our crazy hours. I'm here alone most nights."

"Really? You should let me know sometimes. Maybe we could go grab a drink or something and keep each other company." Jade said with sincerity in her voice.

"Okay, that sounds like a plan." Lynn knew Jade very well. So well that she could tell if she was stressed or going through something that she couldn't handle. Curiosity had her so wired that she decided to just ask. "Jade, have you seen Dr. Hamilton lately?"

"Yeah, you?"

"I have. Actually, I'm going to see him tomorrow but not because I made the appointment. His office called me and said that he wanted to see me tomorrow."

"Really? And you have no idea what it's about?" asked Jade.

"Nah, I just thought maybe it had something to do with you and your family."

"Say what? Me? And my family? Why do you think he'd call you in to talk about me and *my* family? I think that there is a patient-doctor confidentiality thing, even if we are sisters!"

"Yeah, you're right. Guess I'll just have to wait it out," replied Lynn.

"Well, call me tomorrow as soon as you finish with him, and let me know what's up," said Jade.

"Oh, alright, take care, and let's get together soon." Lynn clicked her cell phone off but not before saying bye, and then she sat there for a moment clinching her phone and looking out the bay window of her living room. She texted yes back to the office.

She thought she saw Casey driving up the driveway and wondered if she should share the news with him that the psychiatrist wanted to see her in the morning. She decided against it since she had been flirting with Alex at Starbucks. Somebody may have picked up on the chemistry between them and told the doctor or something. It was not him.

Instead her phone rang. "Hey, baby! What'cha wanna do?" Alex asked Lynn on the phone.

"Go somewhere where there will be just us two," Lynn replied in a very lustful voice. By now the meetings had become more often, and Alex didn't have to beg at all. Lynn was more than willing to meet him. She had even started to rationalize why she was doing what she was doing. She blamed her actions on Casey and his late hours. At one point, she questioned if he was really at work. Her guilt was causing her marriage to crumble.

"How about the bridge over near the Potomac? You know, near the Parkway? I'll be off in about an hour. It'll be dark by then. Just a few minutes, please? I need to see you."

Lynn never could resist Alex when he begged. It actually turned her on. She didn't care if he knew how much she wanted to see him too, even if it was for just a few minutes or an hour. "Okay, I'll see you there around five thirty." Now her challenge was to think up a different lie to tell Casey as to why she wasn't coming straight home. He knew her schedule, and lately, she had been off course and a little evasive. She just hoped he didn't want to stop by her office or ask her to meet him somewhere after work. When she complained about his hours, he promised her that he would do better and try to get home earlier. Lynn only did that to make him think that she wanted him home, hoping that he would not find out that she was getting in a little before him on many nights.

Five-thirty rolled around sooner than Lynn thought. She found herself cleaning up her paperwork and running around like some schoolgirl about to meet her first crush. "Danni," she said, addressing Daniella, her administrative assistant, "would you make sure that everything is in place before you leave? I need to rush out to run some errands."

"Sure, Mrs. Carter, it would be my pleasure." Danni was very obedient and had been trained to simply do her job and to never ask any questions about anything at any time. That was the rule for everyone in the office. Lynn let her staff know that as long as everyone did their jobs and stayed in their prospective lanes, Lynn Baxter and Associates, PC would be very productive. These were times that Lynn was glad that she owned her own business and called her own shots. Lynn Baxter and Associates, PC was a well-known and highly sought after accounting firm in the District. This was another reason that she had to be so discreet when meeting Alex. She was known around town.

Lynn picked up her Louis Vuitton brief case and her cell phone and hustled out of her office, knocking a few papers on the floor in the process. "Oh, snap!" she said to herself.

"Oh, don't worry about it, Mrs. Carter. You go ahead. We'll clean up everything for you," Danni offered, as any efficient AA would.

"Thank you, Danni. I'm sorry. I'm in a hurry to meet someone—I mean, get to a store before it closes. Ahem, if Mr. Carter happens to call, just tell him I'll be home shortly, but I have a few stops to make before I get there."

"No problem, Mrs. Carter. Drive safely now and see ya in the morning."

Lynn got to the elevator, and it seemed as though a thousand people had the same idea. Under her breath, she asked, "What is taking this dang elevator so long?" The elevator wait gave her a little time to think about what she was rushing off to do. How and when did life get to this point? She knew she had a good man who loved her dearly, but it seemed that that was not enough.

Ding!

The elevator door opened, and she pushed herself in with the other hundred folks, making sure that she did not have to wait for the next one.

The traffic in the District was the usual, folks driving like they had bought their driver's license, which slowed things up for Lynn. She had driven out of that parking garage as if she had received an emergency call or something. Some days she wished she didn't drive a Jaguar, especially when she saw folks in those little zip cars. She had already owned just about every foreign car in existence when a coworker suggested she try the Jag. Once she test drove the black one with the biscuit interior, she was sold and drove it off the lot the same day, blasting Teena Marie's latest and Lynn's favorite," Just Us Two." It was in mint condition, but days like this, something smaller would have been a lot better.

In between each traffic light, she was looking in the mirror trying to freshen up her makeup, pushing her hair back, and spraying mint mouthwash into her mouth. There was something mysteriously enchanting about meeting Alex, and she couldn't wait to see him. Finally, she made it to Virginia and slowed up just in time to make the turn for their secret meeting place. She could see Alex leaning on his car door, scrolling through his cell phone. He was so fine to her, and today, he looked extra fine. It appeared that he had changed his clothes before leaving work and was now wearing all black from his baseball cap to his shoes. The tight-fitting sweater displayed every bicep and muscle in his arms, chest, and abdomen. The black Ray Bans covered those beautiful eyes that always looked right through her. The gold cross that hung from his neck was always visible, and she liked that about him.

He stayed at the car and waited for her to park and get out of her car. Lynn's heart was racing. She wasn't sure if she was anxious about seeing him and anticipating what could happen next or if it was the fact that she was doing something that was totally unforgivable if they were ever found out that was exciting to her. Right now, it didn't matter. She put the car in park, stuffed her purse behind the passenger's seat, grabbed her keys, and quickly hopped out of the car.

She could feel his eyes checking her out from her red hat down to her red pumps. He was shaking his head as he slowly put his cell phone in his back pocket as if he couldn't believe what he was seeing heading towards him. As she approached him, she stretched her arms out wide as he fell into them. For a moment, it was just the two of them. It did not matter that there were others down the hill or that cars were passing.

"Baby, we've got to stop meeting like this," Alex whispered in Lynn's ear. He squeezed her tighter and tighter as she began to kick one of her legs up backward. Lynn always seemed to kick her leg back when she was really enjoying an intimate moment.

"I know, but I don't want to stop," she attempted to say as he kissed her on her lips and around her neck. Alex quickly turned her around and leaned her up against his car as his body pressed hard against hers. She had left her jacket in the car which made it easier for him to put his hands under her sweater, touching her skin as he continued biting her lips, face, and neck.

"Let's go to my place," Alex said.

"Babe, you know I can't do that. Not tonight. I have to go home," Lynn said reluctantly.

"How much longer, Lynn? I think I'm falling in love with you." He pushed her back a little so that he could see her face, or at least as best as he could as night was beginning to fall.

"Alex, please, let's just enjoy this moment. You know I'm married. I can't just…" Lynn stopped as if she wasn't sure what to say next. "Come on. Let's walk on the bridge."

She grabbed his arm as he shoved his hands into his pockets, and they began to walk. They both loved the bridge. There was something risqué about it. You could almost feel the currents as they rushed down the Potomac underneath. No matter what season, it was always a little cold and windy.

Once they got to the bridge, they stopped and held each other without saying anything. Lynn laid her head on his shoulder and was intoxicated by the cologne he was wearing. If Alex only knew how torn, she was and how she sometimes wished she could just give it all up and be with him forever.

He lifted her face and began kissing her until every sane sense she was supposed to have disappeared. She kicked her leg up and leaned into him more, pushing him onto the railing of the bridge. As she turned her head, she quickly caught a glance of a shadow at the end of the bridge and stopped kissing Alex.

"What's wrong?" he asked.

"Oh, nothing. I thought I saw someone at the end of the bridge."

"Probably a fisherman or something."

After a while, she put her arms around his waist as he folded his arms and looked away from her.

Lately, their meetings always ended this way. Alex wanted her to leave Casey, but Lynn was not sure if she was ready to make that move. However, she did know that they couldn't continue this rendezvous.

"Can we sit in the car and talk for a while, Lynn?"

These were the times that Lynn hated. Alex would ask to see her for a few minutes, and then the visit would turn into hours when he wanted to talk. Tonight she could not stay long because Casey would be wondering where she was.

"Yes, for a little while," she answered. They held hands as they walked back to the car. He walked her around to the passenger's side of the car and opened the door for her to get in. He drove a 428i BMW, which fit his personality—fast and sexy. The color red with black interior added to his swagger. She watched him walk around the car to get in and couldn't help feel a little guilty, wondering how she was going to say goodnight and leave.

"You know I love you, right? I know it hasn't been that long, but when I'm with you, I don't want to leave, and when I'm not with you, I'm trying to figure out how to be with you. I know you feel the same as I do." He waited for her to respond as he grabbed the leather steering wheel and lowered his head as if to rest it.

Lynn looked straight ahead as night had fallen. All she could think about right then was that she needed to get out of the car and go home with a good lie. As much as she wanted to stay there with Alex, she knew that her place was with Casey.

Alex put his hand on the gear shift to start the car as it had the keyless go feature. On full blast from the CD changer was Teena Marie's song, "Just Us Two." He had been listening to it before he met her earlier. He quickly put the car in reverse and began to back out. The road was covered with gravel, so he was unable to go too fast.

"Alex, what are you doing? Where are you going?" Lynn shouted. "Alex, please, just let me out. We can talk about this later. I promise. I will come by, and we can spend time together. We can talk about our future." He was not listening. It was almost as if he was another person in another world. "Just Us Two" was still playing loudly, and she didn't know if she should reach over and turn it down, fearing that he would be even more upset.

He raced down the Parkway, dodging in and out of lanes as if he were on a speedway, as Lynn pleaded with him to turn around. Lynn was so afraid that she began to cry. She knew that she could not grab the steering wheel because that would put them both in danger. What frightened her, even more, was the fact that Alex was not saying anything. He must have been driving at least eighty-five miles per hour, and the speed limit was only fifty-five. Teena still blared through the speakers.

Lynn couldn't take it anymore. All of a sudden, their favorite song was no longer sounding like love to her. She looked over at all of the high-tech buttons on the console, trying to figure out how to turn off the music.

"Alex! Watch it! Oh, my gosh! What are you trying to do? Kill us?" Lynn cried.

She had not even had time to fasten her seatbelt, and neither had he. She quickly hit the button to turn off the music. "Alex! Please, if you love me like you say you do, please, please, stop the car!" she pleaded with him.

"No! I need you, Lynn!" he screamed just as he passed two cars, nearly sideswiping one.

Just as Lynn raised her arms above her head, he lost total control of the car and slammed into the back of the car in front of him. The airbags deployed as they both fell back into their seats. The car flew into the air and landed on all four tires in the opposite direction than they had been traveling. They were both unconscious.

Chapter 15

A trucker who had seen them at the bridge parking lot and had left around the same time as they had stopped and dialed 911. The emergency personnel arrived on the scene, and they were both taken to the nearest hospital. The trucker stayed behind and answered as many questions as he could about what he had seen. He told the officer that he had seen the woman get out of a black Jaguar that was still parked in the lot near the bridge.

"So, did you notice anything else that might help us determine what exactly happened?" the officer asked the trucker.

"No, sir, I didn't. They looked like they were pretty lovey-dovey, though." He smiled as he began to walk away.

"Sir, may I have your contact information in case we need to ask you more questions?"

"Absolutely. No problem!" The trucker handed the officer a card and pointed to the direction of Lynn's Jag.

The police went back down to check out Lynn's car. She had forgotten to lock it, so they searched the car and found her purse behind the seat where she had left it. They looked for contact information.

"Well, here's her driver's license and registration," said one of the officers on the scene. "I think we should call a tow truck and take her belongings down to the hospital."

Chapter 16

Casey

Lynn and Alex were both pretty banged up and had lost a lot of blood. The officer turned Lynn's purse over to the hospital authorities, but not before taking down all of her contact information. They had checked Alex's wallet, which was found in his back pocket, and noticed that his address was different from Lynn's. Also, on Lynn's front seat was one of Dr. Joe Hamilton's business cards, and on the back, she had written the appointment time for the next day.

The police drove to Lynn's home, hoping to find someone at the residence who knew her. They rang the doorbell and the gentleman who answered the door looked as if he had already heard the bad news.

"Mr. Carter?"

"Yeah, that's me. What's up?" Casey asked the officers.

"May we come in, sir?" one of the officers asked.

Casey stared at them, starting to get anxious as to why they may be there at that hour of the night. "Sure, come on in." He motioned to them. "Have a seat."

"Sir, are you any relation to Lynn Carter?" they began as they sat.

"Yes! I'm her husband! What happened? Is there something wrong with Lynn?" Casey began to pace the floor.

"Well, yes, sir. It appears that she was in an accident and is in the hospital and critical care right now."

Immediately, Casey started looking for his keys. "Which one? General? What happened?" he questioned, almost out the door.

The officers got up. "Sir, please wait. You're upset. Let us drive you."

"No!" As he ran out of the door to get into his car, the officers followed him, but it was too late. He was racing up the road.

Casey parked his car in the emergency lot and

dashed into the hospital. Barely stopping at the receptionist's desk, he was out of breath and had begun to cry a little. "My wife, is she here?" he asked the young lady at the desk.

"Sir, what's your wife's name?"

"Lynn Carter."

"Sure, sir, just sign in here, and you can go through those double doors. Once you get back there, someone can help you find your wife."

Casey quickly signed the form and headed through the doors. He had the nurse walk him back to where Lynn was sleeping. He took a seat beside her bed and took her hand in his. She felt very cold, and she had machines connected to her to help her breathe and keep her heart pumping. She was also connected to several IVs.

"Lynn, speak to me. Please tell me what happened." He dropped his head down onto their hands and began to cry.

In the meantime, Alex had come to enough to hear what was going on with Casey and Lynn in the next bed. When they were brought to the hospital emergency room, the available beds were right next door to each other. Only floor to ceiling gray curtains separated their beds. Tears were streaming down Alex' face. He tried to move, but couldn't. The pain was unbearable. A doctor walked in and asked if there was anything else they could do to make him more comfortable.

"No, I'm just so sorry. Is she okay? Is Lynn gonna be alright? What have I done?" he whispered. Alex wasn't sure of who it was over there talking to Lynn, but he assumed it was her husband, Casey. He whispered so that he would not hear him asking about Lynn.

"Yes, sir," the doctor told Alex. "Lynn is going to be fine. You need to rest now." He pulled the cover over him.

Casey overheard the conversation and was somewhat puzzled. He thought to himself that whoever was talking couldn't have been asking about his wife. At that same moment, Lynn's vitals took a turn for the worse and alerts went off.

"Sir, could you step out for a moment please until we get her settled?"

Casey slowly backed out of the room, looking at his wife, not knowing what to say or think. As he moved out of Lynn's room, he could not help looking at the man who was lying in the bed space next to his wife's. The curtains were partially opened, and he had fallen asleep.

"Hi, I'm Casey, and that's my wife, Lynn, in that room. Can you tell me what happened to her tonight?" He looked at all the nurses gathered around the station, but none of them seemed to want to speak up and give him the news.

"A car accident, sir. She was in a car accident," one of them finally spoke up.

"And the man in the room next to her?" Casey couldn't help but ask.

"Sorry, sir, we're not allowed to give out information on another patient!" The woman wearing the afro looked up from her computer and gave Casey a real dirty look.

He went to the nearest seat to sit down. All kinds of thoughts started running through his mind. Could it be true? Had all his doubts been validated? He had begun to get suspicious in the past months as Lynn's habits began to change.

"Sir, you may join your wife now if you'd like," the attending physician said.

"If I'd like?" he responded. "I'm not sure." Casey took out his cell phone and called Jade and Dr. Hamilton.

Chapter 17

Jade and Porter

"Hello? Casey, is that you?" Jade woke up from a sound sleep, quickly answering the phone before it woke Porter, Addie, and the nanny.

"Yeah, it's Lynn. She's been in a car accident. She's in the hospital. Maybe you'd better get down here; she's gonna need someone." He clicked off his phone, and immediately checked his contacts for Dr. Hamilton's number.

"Dr. Hamilton?" Casey tried not to let him know that he was crying.

"Yes, who is this?" Dr. Hamilton asked, a bit irritated.

"This is Casey, Lynn's husband." Casey choked a

little when he said 'husband.' Lynn's been in an accident, and I really think she needs to see you." Knowing that he was her psychiatrist, he was beginning to feel that maybe there was something mentally wrong with Lynn.

"Really? I'll be right over." All Dr. Hamilton could think about was that he had wanted to see Lynn right away to give her the news he had found out. He knew she was supposed to see him the next day.

Within minutes, Jade, Porter, and Dr. Hamilton had joined Casey at the hospital, and he told them all that he knew. They all rushed into Lynn's room to find her still asleep. Then they returned to the waiting area to comfort and console Casey.

"Was her car messed up pretty badly too?" Jade asked.

"No, actually not at all, not a scratch," Casey answered.

They all looked surprised. "Not a scratch?" Dr. Hamilton asked. "The way she looks now—"

Casey stopped him. "Lynn wasn't driving. Her friend was."

"What friend?" Jade asked angrily. "Lynn doesn't have a lot of friends."

"Well, check with the gentleman in the bed next to hers!" Casey shouted to them.

Dr. Hamilton walked closer to the room, and the moment he saw Alex's face, he gasped and dropped his head. He quickly tried to compose himself because he did not want the others to know that he knew Alex. He thought that he should wait until he talked with Lynn and Alex first.

"What's wrong, Dr. Hamilton?" Jade asked. "Do you know him?

"Yes, Alex is one of my patients. Is he who she was with during the accident?" he asked, concerned.

"Excuse me, folks," said one of the emergency room's attending physicians. "You all will have to take your conversations outside because you're disturbing the patients."

They all walked outside, anxiously waiting to hear what else Dr. Hamilton may have had to say. They sat down in a place where they could all face each other.

Jade sat with Porter to her left and Casey to her right. She started rubbing Casey's back as Dr. Hamilton began to speak.

"Alex Adams is new to this town. He works in downtown D.C. Didn't know that Lynn knew him."

Dr. Hamilton did not reveal what he had recently found out about Alex. He felt that the news would be too devastating, and they were already dealing with too much as it was. He also thought that he'd like to speak to Lynn as her psychiatrist with their and her doctor's permission, if and when she came to.

"Do you mind if I go in and speak with the attending physician about Lynn's condition?" he asked as he hopped up, almost as if he knew the answer would be okay.

"No, go right ahead, Dr. Hamilton," Casey answered in a very solemn tone.

Jade, Porter, and Casey all decided that there was nothing else that they could do at that time and that they should all go home, get a good night's rest, and come back in the morning. Maybe by then Lynn would be able to speak and tell them what happened.

"Good night, Casey. Take care. See you in the morning," Jade said as she hugged him.

"Take care of yourself, man!" Porter wrapped his arm around Casey's back, and they leaned into each other, giving a manly hug.

Dr. Hamilton went back in to see Lynn but not before peeking his head inside to look at Alex. Alex's eyes were open, so Dr. Hamilton decided to stop in and ask how he was doing.

"Alex, how's it going? What happened?" Dr. Hamilton asked as if he knew nothing.

"Dr. Hamilton," Alex said with surprise. "What

are you doing here? Did someone call you?"

"As I was walking by, your curtain was partially opened, and I recognized you." Dr. Hamilton was so baffled by this whole thing now that he wasn't sure of what to say to whom and how much. In his heart, he thought that he should tell both Alex and Lynn about his discovery, but he knew that this was definitely not the time. He was distracted for a moment when he heard movement and talking coming from Lynn's side of the room.

"Yes, she's being moved to room 666. Still ICU. Can you help me with her IV?" The nurses were talking as they were moving Lynn's bed, transferring her upstairs.

He wanted to run out and follow them to Lynn's new room; however, he did not want Alex to know that he knew Lynn, but to his surprise, Alex tried to get out of the bed as he saw her passing by. "Lynn! Lynn! Where are you taking her?"

Dr. Hamilton had to grab him and help him back into the bed. "Alex, what're you doing? You shouldn't be trying to move," he said as he gently pushed him back onto the bed and pushed the call button for a nurse.

"She's a friend of mine. We were in an accident together tonight. It's all my fault!" Alex started to cry but not before Dr. Hamilton sat down in the chair beside his bed.

"Wait a minute, you know Ms. Carter? I mean, the woman that they're moving?" Dr. Hamilton quizzed him.

"Yes. Why? Do you know her?" Alex answered back.

Dr. Hamilton knew that he had better choose his words wisely before he answered because they could come back to haunt him once the truth was revealed.

"Ah, yes, actually I do, but I cannot divulge how we're acquainted. So tell me, Alex, how do you know this lady?" He wasn't sure if he was even ready for the answer but was anxiously awaiting it.

"Well, I met her at the Starbucks around the corner from your office one day, and we just became friends. We started seeing each other, and I have to admit that I've fallen in love with her. So much so, that I was very upset today when we met and started driving recklessly, and that's how we ended up here." Alex started crying again. The good thing was that the nurse was entering the room with some meds that would hopefully put him out of his misery for a while.

"Excuse me, sir," the nurse said to Dr. Hamilton, and then she moved between him and the bed to get to Alex. "I need to give Mr. Adams some medicine to calm him."

"I don't need that! I need to see Lynn!" Alex shouted as he pushed the nurse away.

Dr. Hamilton thought that this would be a great moment to leave and go upstairs to the sixth floor to see if he could visit with Lynn.

"Alex, take care. I'll check on you tomorrow." He didn't wait for Alex to respond but left the room and headed to the elevator situated to the right of the nurses' station. He pressed the button to go up as he pondered what he might say if Lynn was awake. It was actually more a pondering of what he *wouldn't* say at this time.

Once on the sixth floor, no one questioned him as to where he was going or who he was looking for. Maybe because he looked like a doctor or maybe they thought he was somebody's husband or father or brother.

Dr. Hamilton looked left and right and tried to find room 666. The hospital was huge, and the halls seemed extremely long.

Finally, he found room 666. He cautiously tiptoed in, careful not to awaken Lynn if she was asleep and also hoping not to find anyone else in the room. It would be hard to explain who he was and why he was still there at this hour of the night.

Lynn was hooked up to all kinds of machines, and her eyes were tightly shut. They had removed the breathing machine. That was a good sign Dr. Hamilton thought. He spotted a chair next to her bed, quietly walked over to it, and pulled it even closer to the bed. As he sat down, he heard Lynn make a moaning sound as if she may have been in pain. He watched her trying to move her hands. Picking up one of her hands, he began whispering things to her that he did not want any other hospital personnel to hear.

"Lynn, it's Dr. Hamilton. I'm so sorry this happened to you. I have faith that you are going to be fine, and when you do awaken, I have some very important things to share with you. I was going to tell you this tomorrow, which is why I had my staff call you to make an appointment to see me. If only this accident hadn't happened…"

He squeezed her hands, and for a moment, he thought that she had squeezed his hand back. The room was cold, quiet, and still. All you could hear were the drips of the IV and the machines beeping every now and again. Dr. Hamilton kept talking to Lynn for a while because he knew that she couldn't hear him. It was almost a dress rehearsal for him for when he would have to face her and tell her the truth about Alex. It would be harder now that she was married to Casey, and Alex was in love with her. He, of course, did not know if Lynn felt the same way about Alex.

Grabbing her hand again, whispering, he said, "Lynn, you are going to be shocked to hear that Gabe did not die in the plane crash and probably even more devastated to know that Alex is Gabe."

She very weakly squeezed his hand or so he imagined.

Shocked and afraid she may have actually heard him and understood what he was telling her, he shouted, "Nurse, Nurse!" Several nurses rushed into the room. "Yes, sir, what is it?" one of the nurses asked as she moved closer to Lynn but saw that she was still pretty much out of it. "Sir, what happened?"

"Can she hear us talking?" He shoved his hands in his pockets and started pacing.

"No, sir, she is in a very deep sleep right now because of the meds given to her," they answered. "Are you alright, sir?"

Relieved, he dropped his head and answered, "Yes, maybe I should leave now. I'll be back tomorrow."

Chapter 18

"Good Morning, Mr. Carter! How's it going today, sir?" The paperboy was in a good mood this morning but sensed that Casey was not his normal, chipper self.

"Hey, man, what's up?" Casey answered in a very depressed tone.

"Everything okay, Mr. Carter?"

"Nah, not really, but it will be." Casey began to unfold the paper as he closed the door with the other hand. "Have a great day man!" he tried to force a smile. He almost told the paperboy where Lynn was and how she got to the hospital.

His phone started ringing, and he figured it must've been Jade at that hour. Surely enough, it was. "Hey, Jade, what's up?"

"Morning, Casey. How did you rest last night after you got home? I tossed and turned all night. I almost went back down to that hospital to sit with my sister all night, but you know Porter. He almost dared me to leave the house."

"Yeah, right Lynn. I plan to go down in about another hour. I suspect there is no change because the hospital did not call last night or this morning," he said sadly.

"Casey," Jade began, "Last night you said something that stuck with me, long after we got home."

"Yeah, what was that, Jade?" he asked.

"Well, you acted as if you knew the man in the next space from Lynn. Actually, you called him her friend and said that they were in the car together. How is that?" she quizzed him. What made you think that?" Jade was her usual investigative self, but she was not prepared for the answer that Casey was about to give to her.

"Why? How do I know, not think, that he was her friend?" Casey sounded very irritated. "I'll tell you how and why!" he shouted through the phone. "Because I saw them together, on the bridge off the parkway, in Virginia. I was standing at the end of the bridge, and I saw them together. I had followed her from work." Casey clicked off his phone, slammed it down on the floor, and sat down on the sofa. His head in his hands he still could not believe that Lynn had betrayed him.

"Hello? Hello? Casey are you there? Jade could not believe what she had just heard. She turned her phone off and began to cry. Her emotions were running wild. She had so many questions for Lynn, but all she could really think about was why her sister would jeopardize her marriage. Jade couldn't believe that Lynn had fallen in love with another man. There had to be more to this story, and she was going to find out exactly what was going on, but first she needed to call their brothers to let them know that Lynn was in the hospital. They would want to know. Jade needed them now. Lynn needed them now.

Author's Notes and Acknowledgments

Thank you to the ONE who sits high and looks low. I thank God for all the blessings of family and friends who have been with me throughout my life and now my writing journey. I truly believe that HE takes ordinary people and helps them to do extraordinary things.

My wish is that my writings will encourage, educate, entertain, enlighten, inspire and above all bless, someone in a very special way. My testimony is one of authenticity, but yet common with so many other women. The struggle is real.

Many of the themes that are woven throughout my stories focus on real life issues and their impacts on individuals. From bullying on the playground, hazing on high school and college campuses and domestic violence in the home; it is apparent that I am a strong advocate for women and children who have suffered or who are living with domestic violence, and or physical and verbal abuse in some kind of way.

This story is fictitious and about fictional characters, but there is nothing fictional about the issues that they struggle with throughout the story and their relationships. Just Us Two-A Novella is a romantic Realistic Fiction story about twin sisters and their interactions and relationships with people.

Despite their successes in life, they still manage to sabotage their own happiness. They both see a psychiatrist to help them sort out why it is so hard for them to accept, commit and trust in their friendships and relationships; especially with the men in their lives. The characters continue to develop with each new book, and they learn to embrace and own their truth. The psychiatrist helps them to see how much of an impact that living with domestic violence in their family continues to have on them. The struggle is real.

From The National Coalition Against Domestic Violence
www.ncadv.org *Get Help at 1-800-799-7233 (SAFE) or 1-800-787-3224 (TTY)

NATIONAL STATISTICS

- Every 9 seconds in the US, a woman is assaulted or beaten.

- On average, nearly 20 people per minute are physically abused by an intimate partner in the United States. During one year, this equates to more than 10 million women and men.

- 1 in 3 women and 1 in 4 men have been victims of [some form of] physical violence by an intimate partner within their lifetime.

- On a typical day, there are more than 20,000 phone calls placed to domestic violence hotlines nationwide.

- The presence of a gun in a domestic violence situation increases the risk of homicide by 500%.

- Women between the ages of 18-24 are most commonly abused by an intimate partner.

- 19% of domestic violence involves a weapon.

- Domestic victimization is correlated with a higher rate of depression and suicidal behavior.

RAPE

- 1 in 5 women and 1 in 71 men in the United States has been raped in their lifetime.

- Almost half of female (46.7%) and male (44.9%) victims of rape in the United States were raped by an acquaintance. Of these, 45.4% of female rape victims and 29% of male rape victims were raped by an intimate partner.

CHILDREN AND DOMESTIC VIOLENCE

1 in 15 children are exposed to intimate partner violence each year, and 90% of these children are eyewitnesses to this violence.

The life time impact is insurmountable.

Discussion Questions for Readers

1. Does the novella's title adequately describe the story? How was it illustrated?

2. At what point did you decide, you either like or disliked the book?

3. What could have been left out of the story?

4. Was the plot believable?

5. What or who intrigued you about this story?

6. Was the story relevant to any current events?

7. Did the story leave you with any questions that were unanswered?

8. If you were one of the characters, would you have made the same choices he or she did?

9. Did the author seem to appear in the story? If so, who was that character?

10. Were the details described well? Could you visualize the scenes?

11. Should there be a sequel or a spinoff of the other characters?

12. Did the story satisfy your reader's soul or disappoint you?

13. Which sub-character did you want to know more about, and why?

14. If you could say something to one of the characters, what would it be?

15. What did you like or dislike about the writer's style?

Questions from "LitVersations", The Book Conversation Game for serious Readers.

www.litversations.com a must have for every literary book club.

Creator: Debra Owsley

www.ingramcontent.com/pod-product-compliance
Lightning Source LLC
Chambersburg PA
CBHW071326130626
46556CB00004B/1773